Mary Shelley's

FRANKENSTEIN

A retelling by
TANYA LANDMAN

Barrington Stoke

ALSO BY TANYA LANDMAN

Passing for White

One Shot

Jane Eyre: A Retelling

Wuthering Heights: A Retelling

First published in 2023 in Great Britain by
Barrington Stoke Ltd
18 Walker Street, Edinburgh, EH3 7LP

www.barringtonstoke.co.uk

Text © 2023 Tanya Landman

A CIP catalogue record for this book is available
from the British Library upon request

ISBN: 978-1-80090-177-3

Printed by Hussar Books, Poland

*For Isaac and Jack: a version
without "all the rest"*

CAPTAIN WALTON

Such a strange thing has happened!

We have been sailing north on a voyage of discovery for many weeks into waters that are unknown to man. A place unmapped, uncharted.

My ambition is to find out the secrets of the North Pole. I feel destined to make discoveries that will benefit all mankind.

It is summer. Yet last Monday our ship became almost totally enclosed by ice. This dangerous situation was made worse when a thick fog came down. There was nothing to be done but wait and hope for a change in the weather.

At about two o'clock the fog cleared, but to my dismay I saw vast plains of ice stretched out in every direction. The sailors groaned and I grew anxious. At that moment a peculiar sight attracted our attention.

A sled was passing by, half a mile or so away, drawn by dogs. That in itself was shocking. But the stranger thing was that the man driving it was of an oddly gigantic size.

I used my telescope to watch this man's progress until he was lost amongst the distant ice.

His sudden appearance excited me. We were hundreds of miles from any land, or so I believed. But perhaps that was not so? This man looked as if he might be the savage inhabitant of some as yet undiscovered island. But our ship was shut in by the ice. It was impossible for us to follow him and discover the truth.

Just before nightfall the ice broke and the ship was freed. But we did not dare go on our way. Our fear was that we might strike an iceberg in the dark that would rip the hull apart.

I rested in my cabin and in the morning went on deck where I found all the sailors busy on one side of the vessel. They seemed to be talking to someone in the sea. Impossible! But when I looked, I saw a sled very like the one we'd seen the day before.

It had drifted towards us on a large fragment of ice during the night. The dogs that had pulled it were all dead. The man who had been driving the sled was a European who himself was now on the very brink of destruction. The sailors were urging him to come aboard.

He should have been eager – desperate – to be rescued.

But the man asked, "Where are you bound?"

I told him that we were heading north. Only then did he agree to be brought on board.

Good God! I never saw a man in such poor condition. His limbs were near frozen, his body withered from hunger and exhaustion. We wrapped him in blankets and placed him near the stove. He managed to eat a little soup, but it was two days before he spoke again. His name was Victor Frankenstein. His only explanation of what had led him out on such a perilous journey was, "To seek one who fled from me."

Days passed. When I began this voyage, I did not expect to meet anyone who understood my desire to achieve something great. My only companions were common sailors, and I thought I would find no friend on the wide ocean. Yet I discovered that Victor Frankenstein not only understood but shared all my feelings. I saw in him the same thirst for knowledge. I recognised the same flame of ambition in his heart that burns in mine. Yet in him the light has been dimmed by suffering.

Victor Frankenstein told me he was waiting for one event, after which he would die in peace. He has promised to reveal the nature of this event to me. Today, Victor Frankenstein will explain the reasons for his reckless pursuit of the gigantic creature across the ice.

I believe his tale will be strange and harrowing, and intend to record it in his own words.

He begins ...

VICTOR FRANKENSTEIN

1.

I was born to a wealthy and important family of Geneva. For some time I was the only child of parents who were devoted to each other. They loved to travel, and when I was about five years old, we stayed a while in a villa on the shores of Lake Como.

My father was away in Milan when my mother took the opportunity of visiting the poor in a nearby village. My mother was a charitable woman and liked to give help and comfort where she could.

In a shabby peasants' hovel she noticed a golden-haired girl who did not look as if she belonged there. My mother soon discovered the child was the orphaned daughter of a nobleman and decided to adopt her.

On the evening before my mother brought the girl home, she said playfully to me, "I have a pretty present for you, Victor – tomorrow you shall have it."

My father returned from Milan a few days later and found me playing in the hall of our villa with a girl who looked like an angel.

Elizabeth Lavanza was her name. A year younger than myself, she became the beautiful and adored companion of my childhood. We called each other "cousin", but no word can truly express everything that Elizabeth meant to me.

Everyone loved Elizabeth, and I took great pride in their adoration.

I was five years old. I had taken my mother's words literally when she had presented Elizabeth to me as her promised gift. Elizabeth was mine – mine to protect, love and cherish. Until death parted us, Elizabeth was to be only mine.

2.

I had two brothers. Ernest, who was born when I was seven, and William, who was sixteen years my junior. My childhood could not have been happier. We had a town house in Geneva and a villa in Belrive, on the eastern shore of the lake. Elizabeth was a shining light in both places.

She and I lived in perfect harmony. Any difference in our characters only drew us closer together. Elizabeth was calm and contented; I was passionate and intense, with a desperate thirst for knowledge. She delighted in poetry and the wondrous beauty of the landscape around our Swiss home.

Elizabeth was happy to simply admire the mountains and trees and changing seasons, but I craved to discover what caused them. To me the world was a secret that I wanted to find out. I was sure that the hidden laws of nature would one day be revealed to the world by me.

My family lived a quiet life, which suited me very well. It was in my nature to dislike crowds, and I was truly fond of very few people. At school my only real friend was a boy called Henry Clerval. He loved to read stories of danger and adventure, while I longed for scientific discovery. As with Elizabeth, the contrast between Henry's character and my own only made us better friends.

I was thirteen years old when my family took a pleasure trip to a spa town. One day appalling weather meant we had to stay in the inn. It was there I found a book containing the works of Agrippa and settled down to read. As I turned the pages a new light dawned in my mind. Agrippa wrote about wonders and marvels, of being able to turn base metal into gold. He wrote of the philosopher's stone and the elixir that gave everlasting life. Bounding with excitement, I showed the book to my father.

"Agrippa?" Father said with scorn. "Victor, don't waste your time on this trash!"

I would have thrown the book aside if my father had taken the trouble to explain to me that Agrippa's ideas and theories had been proved entirely wrong. If Father had told me that a new and modern scientific system had taken Agrippa's place, I would have read no more of his works.

But my father did not. I was deeply insulted by his scornful tone and so I continued to read. When we returned home, I obtained more of Agrippa's works and many other writers like him. I read them all avidly. I did not care for wealth, but my mind was filled with visions of the glory that would be mine if I could bring the dead back to life and make men live for ever.

And these were not my only visions. I dreamed of raising ghosts and devils. For two years I wallowed in wild, extravagant theories, guided only by my feverish imagination and childish reasoning.

And then, when I was fifteen, I witnessed a terrible storm. It came from behind the mountains, thunder bursting with terrifying violence. As it progressed, a bolt of lightning hit an old and beautiful oak tree which stood twenty yards from the house. A stream of fire burst from its branches. The second the dazzling light vanished I saw the oak had disappeared. Nothing remained of it but a stump. The tree was shattered. I had never seen anything so utterly destroyed.

By chance we had a house guest staying that night, a man who had conducted research into the laws of electricity. He gave an explanation that was new and surprising to me. It overthrew anything I had read in the works of Agrippa and similar writers.

Yet I wasn't delighted by this new discovery. Instead, I became dejected. It suddenly seemed to me that nothing would or could ever be truly known, and that science was a waste of my time. I rejected all my former interests and turned my attention to mathematics.

Looking back, I wonder if my sudden change of course was the result of a guardian angel whispering in my ear in an attempt to avert disaster. But Destiny was too powerful, and she had already decreed my destruction.

3.

At seventeen I was to leave my family and become a student at the University of Ingolstadt. My departure date was fixed, but before it arrived, the first misfortune of my life occurred. This misfortune was, perhaps, a warning of the misery to come.

Elizabeth caught scarlet fever. Her illness was severe, and her life was in great danger. My mother nursed her with such care that Elizabeth was eventually saved. But before she was fit and well again, my mother sickened with the same fever.

Justine was a maid who adored my mother, and she sat by her bedside night and day, day and night. Justine nursed her with the same devotion my mother had shown to Elizabeth. But there was nothing that could be done.

On her deathbed my mother took the hands of Elizabeth and myself and joined them. She said that she hoped we would one day be married, and then my mother died.

I will not describe the grief we felt. I'm sure it can be easily imagined. From whom has the hand of Death not ripped away a loved one?

My mother was dead, but we still lived and still had duties to perform. In the weeks that followed, Elizabeth took my mother's place, running the house quietly and calmly. I was still bound for the University of Ingolstadt.

On the day of my delayed departure they were all there to see me off. My father, my dear friend Henry Clerval, Elizabeth and my brothers, Ernest and William. Such dear familiar faces, and I was to leave them and live amongst strangers!

I was in a state of deep sadness during the long, tiring journey to Ingolstadt. On arrival I spent a solitary night alone in my apartment.

The next morning, I paid a visit to some of the principal professors of the university. Perhaps it was destiny, or perhaps it was a dark angel of destruction that steered my feet to the door of M. Krempe first. He was a coarse, common man but very well informed about the secrets of his science.

He asked me about my previous studies, and I replied carelessly, mentioning Agrippa and the other writers I had once read with devotion.

Krempe stared at me and asked, "Have you really spent your time with such nonsense? Good God! You must begin your studies entirely anew."

He wrote down a list of books and urged me to attend his course of lectures. He also told me about M. Waldman, a fellow professor who would be lecturing on chemistry.

I was not interested in following his advice. Krempe was crude in voice, manner and appearance. Besides, I hated modern science! In past times, alchemists had sought immortality and power. Today's scientists seemed only to want to discredit and mock the glorious visions which had first stirred my interest in the subject.

But two or three days later, I attended M. Waldman's lecture, partly from curiosity and partly because I had nothing else to do. This professor was very unlike his colleague Krempe. When Waldman began to speak, I listened greedily.

"The ancient teachers of science," he said, "promised the impossible and delivered nothing. The modern scientists promise very little. They know that base metal cannot be turned to gold and that the elixir of life is a fantasy. But modern scientists have performed true miracles, with microscopes and crucibles. They have discovered how the blood circulates and the nature of the air we breathe. They penetrate the depths of nature and show how she works in her hiding places. They are capable of gaining new and almost unlimited powers."

The professor's words bewitched me. It was as if my very being was an instrument on which Waldman played. Keys were being touched, chord after chord was being sounded, and soon my mind was filled with one thought, one purpose. *I shall tread the path others have trod before, but then I will go further. I will lead a new way forward. I will explore unknown powers and unfold to the world the deepest mysteries of creation.*

I did not sleep that night. The following morning I paid a visit to M. Waldman and spent the greater part of the day with him. He was generous and kind and showed me around his laboratory, explaining various pieces of equipment and giving instructions on how I should equip a laboratory of my own. After he gave me a list of books, I took my leave.

That day, my fate was sealed.

4.

From that fateful day science became my sole study and my only occupation. I read with passion, attended lectures, met and befriended men of science. I applied myself to my studies so eagerly that the stars often disappeared into the light of morning while I was still working in my laboratory.

My progress was very rapid, and in a matter of months my skill was at the same level as my professors. Two years passed during which I paid no visits home. I was engaged, heart, mind and soul, in the pursuit of the discoveries I hoped to make.

Only those who have experienced the enticements of science can understand them. In other studies you go as far as others have gone before you and there is nothing more to know. But in science there is always something new to marvel at and explore. I was particularly attracted to the structure of the human frame and indeed any animal that lived. I asked myself, where did life begin? When and how did matter change from being inanimate to animate? What was the spark that ignited life?

To examine the causes of life, I began with death. I studied anatomy, but I needed more. I observed the natural decay of the human body, spending many nights in crypts, watching worms devour the wonders of eye and brain. And in the middle of all this darkness I had a sudden revelation that flooded my mind with light.

So many men of science had wanted to discover the origin of life and yet I alone had found the answer. It was so brilliant, so wondrous and yet so simple that I became dizzy. For not only had I discovered the source of life, I was capable of generating it.

I will not say what the answer was or how I came by it. Others may be tempted to follow in my footsteps, and I do not wish to inflict the same miseries I have experienced on any other person. I say only this: I had discovered how to give life to dead matter.

Yet how should I use this power? I debated about the path to take but at last decided to work on the creation of a human being. Stitching together fibres, muscle and veins would be a work of great difficulty and labour. I decided to make my human being of gigantic stature, about eight feet in height, and began to collect materials from dissecting rooms and slaughter-houses. I visited unhallowed graves, collecting bones and probing with unholy fingers the secrets of the human frame.

Excitement drove me onwards like a hurricane. It was intoxicating! A new species would worship me as its creator, I thought, even more grateful to me than a child to its father. And if I could animate lifeless matter, in time I might be able to restore life to those who had been claimed by Death.

With relentless passion I went on, and grew pale and thin with the effort. The moon gazed on my work at midnight. I tortured living animals as I attempted to discover how to animate lifeless flesh. Remembering it now makes me tremble, but back then I was urged forward by a restless, frantic impulse.

The summer months passed as I engaged in this one pursuit. I was blind to the charms of nature and the changing seasons – the leaves had withered before my work drew to a close. Every night I was burdened by the same slow fever, and I became nervous to a painful degree. The fall of a leaf startled me, and I shunned my fellow men as if I was guilty of a crime. Sometimes I was aware of the wreck I had become, but I reasoned that my labour would soon end. I decided exercise and amusement would drive away my disease, and I promised myself both of these when my creation was finally complete.

5.

On a dreary night in November my work came to its conclusion. I collected the necessary instruments and, feeling an agony of fear and dread, infused the spark of being into the lifeless thing that lay at my feet.

It was one in the morning. Rain pattered against the windowpanes and my candle was nearly burned out when I saw the dull yellow eye of the creature open. It breathed hard. Its arms and legs twitched uncontrollably.

How can I describe my emotions at this catastrophe? I had formed the creature with such care! His limbs were in proportion, and I had selected his features as beautiful.

Beautiful? Great God! He was monstrous. His yellow skin barely covered his muscles and the arteries beneath. His hair was glossy black, his teeth pearl white – a horrid contrast with his watery eyes, his shrivelled complexion, his thin, straight lips.

I had worked for two years to give this creature life, depriving myself of rest and health. Now that I had finished, the glory of my dream vanished. Horror and disgust filled my heart. In panic I rushed from the room.

For a long time I paced in my bedchamber. Briefly I slept but was disturbed by the wildest dreams. In them I saw Elizabeth, in the bloom of health, but when I kissed her lips, they became deathly blue. Her features changed, and I was suddenly holding the corpse of my dead mother, while grave worms crawled in the folds of her shroud.

I awoke from my sleep, cold with sweat, teeth chattering. The dim yellow light of the moon lit the creature, which was trying to force its way through my window. Its jaw opened and it uttered strange sounds, one hand stretched out towards me.

I fled outside and passed the night in misery. Morning dawned dismal and wet, and I paced the city streets, sick with fear. At last I came to an inn and paused. A coach was coming towards me and stopped just where I was standing. When the door was opened, out stepped Henry Clerval.

"Frankenstein!" Clerval said cheerfully. "How glad I am to see you! How fortunate you should be here at the very moment of my arrival!"

I was truly delighted to see him. Clerval brought thoughts of my father, of Elizabeth, of home. For a moment I forgot my horror and misfortune and felt nothing but calm and serene joy.

It seemed that after much persuasion Clerval's father had at last allowed him to attend the University of Ingolstadt.

"I am to undertake a voyage of discovery to the land of knowledge," Clerval told me.

I asked after the health of my father and Elizabeth. Clerval assured me that they were well, despite complaining about how rarely they had heard from me. And then he said, "How very ill you look! So thin and pale, as if you have not slept for several nights."

"You are right," I replied. "I have not had sufficient rest lately. But the task which kept me awake is now at an end. I am free."

We walked back towards my apartment. Fearing the monster might still be there I asked Henry to wait at the bottom of the stairs and darted up to my rooms.

The place was empty. Clapping my hands for joy I ran down to fetch Clerval. We breakfasted, but I was unable to stay calm. My pulse raced; I could not keep still.

Clerval noticed the wildness in my eyes and heard my loud, hollow laughter.

"What is the cause of this?" he asked.

"Do not ask!" I said. I put my hands to my eyes for I thought I saw the dreaded monster glide into the room. "Save me! Save me!"

I fell down in a fit and did not recover my senses for a long, long time. A nervous fever kept me in my room for several months. Clerval should have been spending his time in study but instead became my nurse. To protect my family he did not tell them the full extent of my disorder, but I was really very ill. The monster on whom I had bestowed life was forever before my eyes, and I raved constantly.

It was not until the following spring that I began to recover. Gradually, the beauty of the season overcame my gloom. In time I became as cheerful as I had been before I'd become obsessed with my creation. And only then did Clerval place a letter into my hands that had arrived some days before.

6.

The letter was from Elizabeth. It read:

My dearest cousin,

*Clerval writes that you are getting better.
I eagerly hope that you will confirm this in
your own handwriting very soon.*

*Get well, and return to us. You will
find a happy, cheerful home and friends
who love you dearly. Your father's health
is good, and he wants only for you to be
happy.*

*How pleased you would be to see Ernest!
He is sixteen now, full of activity and spirit,
and wanting a military career. And I wish
you could see darling William. He is very
tall for his age with laughing blue eyes,
dark eyelashes and curling hair. When he*

smiles, two dimples appear on each rosy
cheek.

Apart from the growth of your brothers,
little has altered here. The blue lake and
the snow-capped mountains never change.

Elizabeth went on to relate the births, marriages
and deaths of various friends and neighbours. She
also mentioned that Justine – the maid who had
nursed my dying mother so faithfully – had come
back to the house after having been away for a long
period looking after her own parent. Justine was
more sister than servant to Elizabeth, so her return
was especially welcome.

Elizabeth's letter concluded:

Write back, dearest Victor – one line, one
word will be a blessing. Ten thousand
thanks to Henry for his kindness, his
affection and his many letters: we are
sincerely grateful. Take care of yourself
and I beg you, please write!

I obeyed instantly, but even the slight exertion of
writing a short note tired me. Yet I was improving.

And in two weeks more I was able to leave my chamber.

My first duty was to introduce Clerval to the professors of the university. I had developed an aversion to the very name of science, and the sight of my instruments renewed my nervous agony. Seeing this, Henry had removed all my apparatus from my laboratory. He had even changed my apartment when he saw my dislike for that room.

But Clerval could not protect me from the professors. Waldman praised with kindness and warmth the progress I had made in my studies. He meant to please, but he tormented me. And M. Krempe's coarse, blunt compliments gave me even more pain.

"Damn the fellow!" Krempe cried. "Why, M. Clerval, Frankenstein outstripped us all with his achievements!"

Clerval had never understood my taste for science. His pursuits were the opposite of mine. He came to the university intending to master languages, and I was easily persuaded to join Clerval in his studies.

Summer passed pleasantly away in this manner. The plan was for me to return home for the autumn, but this was delayed first by a series of minor accidents and then by the snows of winter.

Spring came late. The month of May had already begun, and every day I expected the letter that would fix the date of my departure. Until then Henry and I filled the time walking in the hills, for my health had finally been restored and Henry rejoiced to see it.

Dearest Clerval! Henry was an excellent friend! How sincerely he loved me. My selfish ambitions had cramped and narrowed me. But his gentle affection warmed my heart and opened my senses once more. Under his care I became the same happy creature who a few years ago was loved by all and knew no sorrow.

7.

A letter arrived from my father. I thought it would simply inform me of the date I was to return home. Imagine my shock when I read:

William is dead! The sweet child whose smiles delighted my heart is murdered!

I will not attempt to console you but will simply relate what happened.

Last Thursday we went walking at Plainpalais – myself, Elizabeth and your two brothers. William and Ernest ran on ahead. At dusk the two boys were nowhere in sight. Elizabeth and I sat and waited for their return, and Ernest came back, but William did not. They had been playing and William had run away to hide himself.

We searched until nightfall, and then we thought that perhaps William had returned to the house. He had not. We

took torches and continued our search.
About five the following morning I found
my boy stretched out on the grass, livid and
motionless. The print of the murderer's
finger was on his neck.

When I carried William home, Elizabeth
cried aloud that she herself had killed him
and then fainted. When revived, she wept
and told me that William had begged her
to let him wear the little painting of your
mother. Elizabeth had gladly lent it to
him. The painting was valuable and now
it is gone. Stolen. Theft was surely the
reason for William's murder, which is why
Elizabeth now blames herself. Come home,
dearest Victor. You alone can console her.
She weeps continually.

Thank God your mother did not live to
witness this!

My journey home was miserable. I wished to hurry
at first, but the closer I got to my native town, the
slower my progress became. So many feelings
crowded into my mind! I had not been home for so
long! Fear of the changes I would find there finally
overcame me, and I stopped altogether at Lausanne.

The view of the lake and the mountains calmed me, and after two days I continued my journey. But night was drawing in, and by the time I reached Geneva the gates were already shut. I had to stay the night in a village outside the city wall.

Unable to rest I decided to visit the spot where poor William had been murdered. I could not pass through the town, so I crossed the lake to Plainpalais in a little boat. During the short voyage, lightning began to strike the summit of Mont Blanc. The storm approached rapidly, and on landing I climbed a low hill to watch its progress.

The rain began to fall as I walked on. Vivid flashes of lightning dazzled my eyes like vast sheets of fire, so beautiful yet so terrifying.

"William!" I called aloud. "Angel! Behold! The whole of nature weeps for you!"

As the words left my mouth I noticed a shape in the gloom. A flash of lightning illuminated a person of gigantic stature. It was the hellish monster to whom I had given life! What was that devil doing here?

Could he be the murderer of my brother?

As soon as the idea crossed my mind I was sure it was the truth. I shivered so violently I had to lean against a tree for support.

Of course he was William's murderer! No human could have killed such a beautiful child!

Another flash of lightning showed the monster far away from me now, climbing the sheer rockface of the mountain. In moments he reached the summit, then disappeared.

Two years had passed since I had given him life. Was this his first crime? Had I let a villain loose upon the world who delighted in bloodshed? No one can imagine the anguish I suffered that night.

When day dawned, I set off to my father's house knowing that if I spoke of what I had seen and done, no one would believe me. I had suffered a nervous collapse. Any mention of a gigantic creature would be taken as the ravings of a lunatic. And even if I could persuade anyone to go in pursuit of the monster – what would be the use? He had scaled a mountain in moments – who could possibly catch up with him?

I arrived home at five in the morning. My family were sleeping, and I told the servants not to disturb them.

Ernest was the first to wake, and when he saw me, his tears began to fall.

"Elizabeth accuses herself of causing William's death," Ernest told me, his voice cracking with sorrow. "But since the murderer has been caught—"

"Caught!" I exclaimed. "How? When? It would be easier to catch the wind! I saw him – he was free last night."

My brother looked at me, confused. "I don't know what you mean," he replied. "Justine is the murderer."

I was astounded. "Justine?" I said. "Is she accused? No one believes that, surely?"

But it seemed they did.

Ernest informed me that the same morning William's body had been found, Justine had suddenly become ill and had taken to her bed. Another servant had tidied her clothes and discovered the painting of my mother in Justine's pocket. The servant had gone straight to the magistrate.

I shook my head. This was nonsense!

"I know the murderer," I said. "Justine is innocent."

At that moment my father entered the room.

Ernest told him, "Victor says that he knows the murderer."

"As do we all," my father replied heavily. "I had not thought Justine capable of such wickedness."

"She is innocent," I said again.

Elizabeth heard my words as she came down the stairs.

"Everyone believes Justine is guilty," she told me. "Not only have we lost our darling boy, but this poor girl is to be torn away from us by an even worse fate. But she is not a murderer and surely cannot be condemned! She will not. Your arrival fills me with hope. Victor, you will find out the truth."

I knew that Justine and indeed every other human being on earth was guiltless of this murder. But I could not tell anyone why. Instead, I told Elizabeth to have faith in the justice of law. I assured her that an innocent woman like Justine would not be convicted of such a crime. I comforted my cousin as best I could, but there was little to be said and nothing to be done.

Justine's trial began later that day.

8.

Justine's trial was a cruel mockery of justice, and watching it was torture for me.

Justine was dressed in the black of mourning. Sorrow made her look utterly beautiful. She entered the court, and when she saw my family, a tear dimmed her eye, but she remained perfectly calm.

Witnesses were called. Several facts conspired against Justine. She had been out the whole night of the murder. Towards morning, Justine had been seen by a market woman not far from where William's body had been found. When the woman asked what Justine was doing there, her answer was mumbled and confused.

Justine returned to our house at about eight o'clock, and when the other servants asked her where she'd been, she told them she had been out looking for William. On seeing his body she fell into violent hysterics and kept to her bed for several days.

When the painting of my mother that was found in Justine's pocket was produced, a murmur of horror rippled around the court.

Justine was called to defend herself. She struggled with tears as she told her story.

She had spent the evening at her aunt's house, she said. When she was returning, she had passed a man who asked her if she had seen the missing child. Learning that William had disappeared Justine then spent so many hours looking for him that the gates of Geneva were shut when she tried to return.

The weather worsened, and she took shelter in a barn. Justine had been awake almost all night, sleeping only for a few minutes before dawn. The sound of footsteps had woken her, so she rose and again went in search of my brother. If Justine had been near the place where William's body was found, it was without her knowing, she said. Her reply to the market woman who'd questioned her had been confused because Justine was exhausted and anxious.

Justine had no explanation for how the painting had got into her pocket. It was this one fact that condemned her.

Witnesses were called who had known Justine for years and knew her to be a good woman. But they were so appalled by the crime she seemed to have committed they were reluctant to say anything in her favour. Elizabeth herself took to the witness stand and spoke passionately in Justine's defence, but the public fury was so strong by then that Elizabeth's pleas made no difference.

I could see the judges' minds were already made up, and I rushed out of the court in agony. Justine's sufferings were not equal to mine. Justine was at least innocent, but I felt as if fangs of guilt were tearing into my flesh.

I passed a night of utter misery. In the morning I went to the court. The verdict had been given. Justine was condemned.

The very next day she went to her execution and became the second helpless, hapless victim of my dark arts.

9.

Justine died. She rested. And I was alive. The blood flowed in my veins, but the weight of regret and despair pressed on my heart, and nothing could remove it. I could not sleep. For weeks I wandered like an evil spirit. I had committed deeds of such horror. How had it happened? I had begun life with such good intentions. I had tried to make myself useful to my fellow beings. Now all was in ruins. Guilt carried me into a hell that no words can express. My only comfort was to isolate myself in deep, dark, deathlike solitude.

After my family had retired for the night, I often took the boat and passed many hours on the water. Sometimes, with sails set, I was carried by the wind. At other times I rowed to the middle of the lake and then let the boat drift as I allowed misery to overcome me.

I was often tempted to plunge into the silent lake and let the waters close over my head. But I was stopped by thoughts of Elizabeth, of my father and my brother. How could I leave them exposed to the demonic monster I had let loose amongst them? For I had a strange feeling that William's murder was simply the first of his crimes, and I lived in daily fear that the creature would commit some new evil. Hatred towards him and a desire for revenge consumed me.

Our house mourned. My father's health was deeply shaken. Elizabeth was sad and downcast. The world that had seemed to her so full of wonder and joy had become a place of injustice and cruelty. As for myself, nothing could save my soul from sorrow – not even all the tenderness of friendship and the beauty of the earth. I was lost in a fog that nothing could penetrate.

Some days despair weighed on me so heavily I could barely move. On others a whirlwind of passions drove me to violent exercise. During one of these restless periods, I left my home for the Alpine valleys.

I made the first part of my journey on horseback. Later, I hired a mule which was more sure-footed on the rugged ground. It was August, two months after the death of Justine, and the weather was fine. I rode through a ravine beside a plunging river, and the great weight on my spirits lightened a little. Crossing a bridge I began to ascend a mountain.

Something long forgotten came to me with each turn in the road – a tingling sense of pleasure. The wind whispered soothing sounds; Mother Nature seemed to be telling me to weep no more.

At last I reached the village inn where I intended to stay a few days. From the window of my room I could see the sunlight play above Mont Blanc and listen to the rushing river. It was like a lullaby, and when I placed my head upon the pillow, sleep crept over me, the blessed bringer of unconsciousness.

10.

I spent the following day roaming among mountains and glaciers. The glorious scenes did not remove my grief, but they softened it. Once more I slept peacefully at night.

But the next day a deep, dark sadness clouded every thought. The rain poured in torrents, and thick mist covered the summits of the mountains. Yet what were rain and mist to me? I took my mule, determined to climb a nearby mountain.

The winding path was cut into the rock. The landscape I passed was harsh and desolate, the trees broken, the ravines full of snow.

It was nearly noon when I reached the summit. For some time I sat on a rock overlooking a sea of ice. A mist covered the peaks of the surrounding mountains, but soon a breeze blew the clouds away. Leaving the mule I walked onto the uneven surface of a glacier that rose and fell like waves on a stormy sea.

It took me two hours to cross the glacier. On the opposite side was a bare mountain. When I turned back, I could see Mont Blanc rising majestically in the far distance. This magnificent sight swelled my heart, and I said aloud, "Spirits, allow me this happiness! Or else take me away from the joys of life."

The moment the words left my mouth I saw a distant figure coming towards me at superhuman speed. It bounded over crevices in the ice which I had tiptoed across with care. As it got closer I saw it was not a spirit come to carry me away to the blessed oblivion of death. His gigantic stature made a mist come over my eyes, and I felt faint. I trembled with rage and horror as the monster I had created drew near. His face showed both bitter torment and cruel spite. His unearthly ugliness was too horrible for human eyes.

"Devil!" I cried. "Do you dare approach? Do you not fear the revenge I will wreak on your miserable head?"

"You wish to kill me. I expected this," said the monster. "All men hate those who are wretched, and I am more wretched than any living thing. You are my creator. You gave me life. You owe a duty to me, yet you detest and reject me. But we are bound with ties that can only be dissolved by death. Know this – if you fulfil your obligation to me, then I will leave you and the whole of mankind in peace. But if you refuse, I will spill the blood of your friends until Death himself can stomach no more."

I sprang at him enraged, but he dodged me easily.

"Be calm!" the monster ordered. "Hear me. Have I not suffered enough? My life may be painful to me, but I will defend it. Remember you have made me more powerful than yourself. But I will not go to war against you. I will be mild and gentle if you will do the task I ask of you. I am your creation: I should be your Adam, but instead I am your fallen angel, your Lucifer, whom you drive from Heaven into the deepest depths of Hell. I was good and kind once. Misery has made me a devil. Make me happy and I shall be an angel once again."

Once more I tried to fight and he escaped me. Once more I cursed him and told him to be gone. Once more the devilish monster begged for my pity and compassion.

"My soul once glowed with love and humanity," he said. "But now I am alone, miserably alone. You, my creator, hate me. What hope do I have from your fellow creatures who owe me nothing? If the whole of mankind knew of my existence, they would arm themselves and destroy me. Why should I not hate those who detest me? But it is in your power to change this.

"Listen to my tale. It is a long one, and the freezing cold of this place will injure you. There is a hut upon the mountain. Let us go there. You shall hear my story and then decide my fate. The choice is yours. Should I leave for ever the neighbourhood of man and lead a harmless life? Or should I become the torment of your fellow creatures and be the author of your ruin?"

The monster led the way across the ice, and I followed. For the first time I did indeed feel the duty of a creator. I should at least try to make him happy before I complained of his wickedness.

It began to rain again. We entered the hut, the monster with an air of triumph and I with a heavy heart. I sat myself beside the fire my repulsive companion lit, and I listened as he began his tale.

THE CREATURE

11.

The start of my life is confused and indistinct. Sensations overwhelmed me. Sight. Sound. Smell. Taste. Touch. All at the same time. Blood surged in my veins, my limbs twitched, cold air was sucked into my lungs. I moved. How? Where? Knowing nothing, I stumbled in darkness.

After some time, light began to press on my eyes. It grew stronger. So strong it hurt. The heat tired me. I looked desperately for a shaded place and came at last to a forest where I lay down beside a stream. There I rested until hunger and thirst began to torment me. I ate the berries that hung from trees and drank from the stream. Lying down once more I was overcome by sleep.

It was dark again when I woke, and I was frightened. I had covered myself with clothes before I left your apartment, but they were no protection against the cold night air. I was a helpless, shivering, miserable wretch. I knew nothing. I could see nothing. Pain consumed me and I wept.

But soon a gentle light appeared over the heavens, and I saw a radiant disc among the trees. I gazed at it with wonder. It was the moon, of course, but I had no word for it. I had no words for anything, and so there was nothing in my mind but confusion.

Days and nights passed. I had no one to help or guide me, but bit by bit I made discoveries about the world around me. I realised that the pleasant sounds I heard came from the throats of little winged animals. I tried to copy them, but the ugly roar that came from my mouth scared me into silence again.

One day I found a fire which had been left by wandering beggars. I was so cold that in my joy I thrust my hand into the embers. Such terrible pain! How could the thing that warmed me also cause me to scream in agony?

I saw that the fire ate wood and so I collected branches to feed it. I kept it alive and so did not perish from the bitter cold. But as the days passed and the weather grew even colder, food became scarce. I was torn with pangs of hunger and forced to leave the forest in search of something to eat.

I did not fare well in the world of men. The first human being I met was an old man who was preparing his breakfast in what I suppose was a shepherd's hut. When he saw me, he screamed and ran away, abandoning his food. I ate it and went on.

I crossed open country and many fields and came at last to a village. It seemed miraculous to me. There were little huts, small cottages, grand and stately houses all set out in rows. Vegetables and flowers grew in neat gardens. I heard singing and laughter, and the air was thick with delicious smells. I was hungry by then and so approached a cottage. But I had barely reached the door when the woman inside saw me and fainted. Her terrified children screamed, and their noise alerted the rest of village. Some fled. Others attacked, hurling stones and anything else they could find at me. I was soon bruised and bloodied, wounded in body and soul. There was nothing I could do but run away.

That night I escaped the cold weather and even colder hearts of mankind in an empty hovel next to a remote cottage. I did not realise until the next day that the dwelling was occupied.

I stayed hidden in the hovel, but by putting my eye to a chink in the wall I was able to see the inhabitants. There were three residents living in a cottage that was clean but very bare of furniture. A young man and woman, and a silver-haired, much older gentleman. They seemed so mild mannered after the screaming villagers, speaking softly and giving each other tender smiles. And yet I could sense the sadness that hung over them and felt compassion stirring in my heart.

The young man soon left the house carrying tools and set off across the fields. Later, he returned with wood for the fire. The young woman tidied the cottage while the old gentleman took up an instrument and began to play. The tune was sweeter than birdsong, and I gazed at him with wonder.

After some time, the old man began to play a different tune, which was also sweet but sounded so sorrowful it drew tears from the eyes of the young woman. He took no notice until she sobbed audibly and then, when he spoke to her, she knelt at his feet. He raised her up, embraced and then smiled at her with such warmth and kindness that my senses were overwhelmed.

I felt a mixture of pain and pleasure that I had never before experienced, not from hunger or cold, or warmth or food. I turned away, not knowing how to cope with such powerful new emotions.

12.

That night I could not sleep. I longed to join these gentle people, but what I had suffered at the hands of the villagers made me wary. I decided to stay in the hovel, watching them, trying to find out more.

The following day passed much the same as the one before. The young man worked out of doors, the girl inside. I soon realised the old gentleman was blind. He spent his time either playing his guitar or in quiet contemplation.

I often saw the young woman and the young man weep. I could see no reason for their sorrow, but I was deeply affected by it. If such lovely creatures were unhappy, it was less strange that I should be so wretched, since I was an imperfect thing. Yet why were these gentle beings unhappy? They had a delightful house, a fire to warm them and food to eat. They enjoyed each other's company, exchanging such looks of affection. What did their tears mean?

A considerable period of time passed before I discovered that the reason for their sorrow was poverty. Their diet seemed glorious to me but consisted only of vegetables from the garden and milk from one cow, who gave very little in winter. They often felt the pangs of hunger, and several times I saw the two youngest put food before the old man yet eat nothing themselves.

Their kindness moved me. Sometimes during the night I had stolen some of their food for my own consumption. But when I saw how they suffered, I satisfied myself only with berries, nuts and roots which I gathered from the nearby wood.

I had seen that the young man spent a great deal of time cutting wood for the fire. To assist them, I took his tools at night and brought back sufficient fuel to last them several days.

The first time I did this they were astonished. The young man did not go to the woods that day but spent his time making repairs on the cottage and tending to the garden.

Little by little I made more discoveries. They seemed able to communicate feelings and thoughts to one another by emitting sounds. I longed to master this for myself. In time I learned the words for "fire", "milk", "bread" and "wood". I learned the names of the people. The old man had but one name – "father". The young woman was called "sister" or "daughter" or "Agatha". The young man "Felix", "brother" or "son".

I yearned to know and understand more, and so I spent the whole winter studying my neighbours. I joyed in seeing them and in hearing the old man play his guitar. But I was puzzled when Felix read aloud to his father and sister. I began to understand that he uttered the same sounds when he read as when he talked. I guessed therefore that there were signs for speech on the page which he understood.

I wished to understand these signs myself, but how was such a thing possible? I could not even attempt it until I spoke their language. I knew myself to be a monster. I had seen my reflection in a puddle, and the sight of my own face had horrified me. But if I could talk with these kind, gentle neighbours, might they overlook my appearance?

Months passed. At last the sun melted the snow. Plants sprang up in the garden, and food became more plentiful. I had fallen into a routine. By day I observed my friends. By night I went into the woods to gather food for myself and firewood for them. I also undertook whatever tasks I could see that needed doing – sweeping a path, repairing a fence, clearing the ground of weeds. When they woke and saw, they uttered the words "good spirit".

In so many ways I made life easier for them, yet they still remained sad. Felix, especially, was downcast. I foolishly thought that it might be in my power to restore their happiness. My imagination formed a thousand pictures of how I would present myself to them. They might at first be disgusted by my appearance but, with my gentleness and soft speech, I would win their favour and then their love.

13.

One fine spring morning my neighbours were surprised by a knocking on their cottage door. A veiled lady on horseback was outside. She uttered just one word when the door was opened.

"Felix?"

As he stepped into the light she threw back her veil and I saw a creature of angelic beauty.

Sorrow fled from Felix. Ecstatic joy flooded his face.

"Safie!" he cried. "My sweet Arabian!" He lifted her down from her horse and they went into the cottage together where Agatha and her father welcomed the stranger with delight.

At once joy took the place of sadness in the cottage, but I soon realised that Safie had a language of her own. When she spoke, my neighbours did not understand her words any more than she understood theirs. However, she was eager to learn. As was I.

In the days and weeks and months that followed they taught Safie to speak and then to read and write in their language. I too learned. When Felix read aloud in the evenings, geography, history and science were all revealed to me. I learned of the Greeks and the Romans and the fall of their civilisations. I marvelled that mankind could be so virtuous and magnificent and yet also be so vicious and evil.

As Felix read I learned of the system of society, of the divisions of property, of immense wealth and grinding poverty; of rank, descent and nobility. I discovered that what human beings value most are noble blood and vast riches. A man might be respected with only one of these assets but needed both to be considered important.

And what was I? I was ignorant of my creation and my creator. I had no friends, no money, no property. Besides that, I was deformed and revolting. What was I? I wondered. I was stronger and taller and faster than a man, I could live on a poorer diet, I coped with extremes of hot and cold with greater ease. But there was no one else like me. Was I then an unnatural monster, a blot upon the earth?

I learned other lessons too. The difference between the sexes. The birth and growth of children. How both father and mother cherish their offspring. Of the love that exists between brothers and sisters and cousins.

But where were my relations? No father or mother had lovingly held me as an infant or marvelled as I grew. My past life was blank; I had always been as I was in height and proportion. The question again came to me – what was I?

These thoughts were an agony to me. Knowledge is such a strange thing! It clings to the mind like moss to a rock. I wished sometimes that I could shake off all thought and feeling, but the only way to achieve that was to die.

14.

Some time passed before I learned the history of my friends (for in my innocence, that was what I called them).

The name of the old man was De Lacey. They were a noble, wealthy French family who had lived in Paris until Safie's father, who was a Turkish merchant, had caused their ruin.

Safie's father had been wrongly accused of a crime and sentenced to death. All of Paris had known it was his religion rather than his guilt that had condemned him. But only Felix had been outraged enough to do anything. He vowed to free the merchant. In the course of planning his escape, Felix met, fell in love with and was betrothed to the merchant's daughter, Safie.

The night before the execution, Felix freed Safie's father from his prison. Felix, Safie and her father then fled from Paris. Slowly, secretly they made their way to Italy.

The government of France were outraged by the merchant's escape. When they discovered Felix's plot, they threw his father and Agatha into jail. News of their imprisonment reached Felix and he hurried back to Paris to confess, thinking that his innocent father and sister would be freed.

They were not. All three De Laceys were jailed for five months until their trial. After that, their fortune was confiscated and they were driven out of their native country.

Now Felix was reduced to poverty, Safie's father turned his back on good feeling and honour. He decided he did not wish his daughter to be married to a Christian and intended to return with her to Turkey. It was in the rented German cottage where they now lived that Felix had learned of the merchant's treachery. He thought he would never see his beloved Safie again, and it was this that had made him so sad these past months.

But Safie had an independent mind. When she discovered what her father planned, she was furious. She took the jewels and money that belonged to her and fled. After a long and difficult journey, Safie finally arrived safely at her lover's door.

15.

In August that year, by chance I found a leather bag abandoned in the woods that contained clothes and several books. I took these eagerly, for I had learned to read by then. I returned to my hovel and continued to study. I read volumes of history. Who was I? I asked myself. What was I? Where had I come from? What was my destination? These questions circled in my head every waking moment.

I looked for answers in *Paradise Lost*. I read it as I had the other volumes – not as a work of the imagination but as a true history. Every feeling of wonder and awe moved in me as I learned of an omnipotent God warring with his creatures.

Like Adam, I was alone. Yet Adam had sprung perfect and whole from the hands of his Creator. Adam had been cared for by Him. I was perhaps more like Satan. For like Satan I too often felt the bitterness of envy when I looked upon my happy friends. And yet, when Satan was cast out of Heaven, even he had companions.

When I fled from the laboratory, I had snatched your journal, Victor Frankenstein. Now, for the first time, I was able to read it. I studied your account of the months that led to my creation. I learned of my origin and the disgusting circumstances of it. I felt sick as I read, and I cursed you. Why did you make a monster so hideous that you turned away in disgust? God made Man in his own image. You made me a filthy mockery of yours.

In the hours of darkness my thoughts tormented me. But in the light of day I convinced myself that the De Laceys would be compassionate towards me. Surely they would not, could not, turn away someone who asked only for friendship? One day, when the time came, I would talk to them.

Several changes had taken place in the cottage. Felix and Agatha were now assisted by servants and spent more time talking and laughing with Safie than working. They were not rich, but they were content. Their feelings were blissfully calm, whilst mine became stormier every day. My increased knowledge and understanding of the world confirmed me as an outcast. My hopes to befriend them vanished each time I looked at my own reflection.

Autumn came. The leaves fell. But the De Laceys' happiness did not fade with summer's passing. I yearned for their protection and kindness but still did not approach them. The winter advanced. When an entire year had passed since I awoke to life, I finally fixed upon a plan.

I would enter the cottage when the blind old man was alone. If I could gain his goodwill, he might persuade the others to tolerate me.

One day Safie, Agatha and Felix departed on a long country walk. My heart beat fast: this was the moment. The servants were gone. All was silent.

Faint with fear, I knocked upon the cottage door.

"Come in," the old man called.

I entered. "Pardon my intrusion," I said. "I am a traveller in need of rest. May I sit a few moments by your fire?"

He welcomed me in. I sat in silence until the old man asked if I was French.

Choosing my words with care I replied that I had been educated by a French family. He asked where I was travelling to, and I told him I was going to claim the protection of friends who had never seen me and knew nothing of me.

"I am full of fears," I said. "For if I fail, I am an outcast in the world for ever."

"The hearts of men, when free of prejudice, are full of love," he replied. "If these friends are good people, do not despair."

"They are kind and good, but they will be prejudiced against me. Where they should see a kind friend, they will behold only a revolting monster."

"Can you not change their minds?" asked the old man.

"I am about to try," I said. "And yet I feel so many terrors! I tenderly love these friends. I have been doing them daily kindnesses, unknown to them. But they will think I wish to injure them, and it is that I must overcome."

"Where do they reside?" he asked.

"Near this spot."

The old man paused awhile and then said, "If you will tell me the whole of your tale, I may perhaps be of use. There is something in your words that tells me you are sincere. I am a poor man, banished from my own country, but it will give me pleasure to help a fellow creature if I can. May I know the names and residence of your friends?"

This was the moment that would either rob me of happiness or give me bliss for ever. I began to tremble and sob just as I heard footsteps outside. I took the hand of the old man and cried, "Now is the time! Save and protect me! You and your family are the friends I seek. Do not desert me in my hour of need!"

"Great God!" exclaimed the old man as I clung to his knees. "Who are you?"

The door opened. Felix, Safie and Agatha entered. It is impossible to describe their looks of horror. Agatha fainted. Safie fled. Felix darted forward and ripped me from his father. He struck me with his stick.

I could have torn him limb from limb. But my heart had sunk into bitter sickness. I was overcome by pain and anguish. In the noise and confusion I escaped from the cottage and hid once more in my hovel.

16.

When night came, I left my hovel and gave way to howling anguish. I was a wild beast raging through the wood while the cold stars looked down and mocked me. Hell burned in my belly, and I wished to wreak havoc and destruction. No one pitied me, so why should I pity anyone? I declared war on all mankind, and especially upon the creator who had condemned me to this unbearable misery.

When the sun rose, I hid myself in the wood. Light and clear air soothed me a little, and I began to wonder if the situation was beyond repair. De Lacey had been sympathetic to me. If I returned to the cottage, if I spoke to the old man once more, perhaps even now he would help me?

I slept, but my dreams were of Felix, tearing me from his father's feet. I awoke exhausted and, finding that it was already night, went in search of food. When my hunger was appeased, I returned to the hovel. All was quiet in the cottage, and I sat waiting for the light of dawn when they would rise.

The hour passed, and they did not appear. The cottage remained cold and dark and silent. I trembled, thinking some disaster had occurred. The sun was high in the sky when I saw Felix approaching with another man – his landlord, I believe. He said, "Felix, you will lose three months' rent and the produce of your garden. Will you not reconsider?"

"We can never live here again," replied Felix, shivering violently. "My father's life is in danger. My wife and sister will never recover from their horror. We must leave this place at once."

Moments later Felix was gone. I never saw any of the De Lacey family again.

I allowed myself to be carried away by a rising tide of despair and revenge. I vented my fury on objects since I was unable to injure anything human. I gathered combustible materials and placed them around the cottage. That night I destroyed every scrap of cultivation in the garden. I tore down fences, ripped up paths. A fierce wind arose, and I lost all reason. I lit a dry branch and screamed as I fired the straw and heath and bushes which I had piled by the cottage walls. The wind fanned the flames. I waited until I was sure that no part of that detestable building could be saved, then I left the scene.

The world was before me. But, hated and despised as I was, where could I go?

The name of Victor Frankenstein crossed my mind. My father, my creator. I felt nothing for you but hatred. Yet who else would help me? You had given me life. Surely from you I could hope for just and fair treatment?

I had learned from your journal that your home was in Geneva. I knew from the lessons Felix had given to Safie where Geneva was.

My travels were long and my sufferings intense. I moved only at night while nature decayed around me. Everything was bitter and cruel and cold. Rain poured. Snow fell. Rivers were frozen. I found no shelter.

By the time I reached Switzerland the spring had come. One day I found that my path lay through a deep wood and I continued to walk after the sun had risen. The warmth and beauty of spring returned sensations of gentleness and pleasure to me. I dared to be happy until I came to a deep and rapid river. Here I heard the sound of voices, and a young girl came running, laughing, as if she was playing a game of chase.

When she slipped and fell into the water, I leaped from my hiding place and dragged her from the raging torrent. I was trying to revive her when a man appeared. He tugged the girl from my arms and fled with her through the wood. Stupidly, I followed. Aiming his gun at me, he fired.

My flesh and bone shattered. It was agonising. I had saved the life of a child, and this was my reward? Kindness had been in my heart a moment before, but now hellish rage took its place.

For some weeks my wound meant I couldn't leave the woods. When I did go on, no bright sun or gentle breeze could soothe me. In two months I reached the shores of Lake Geneva, found a hiding place and thought about how to approach you, my creator.

I was sleeping when a beautiful child came running into the recess where I was hidden. Waking, I gazed at him. I was seized by the idea that this little creature was without prejudice. He was an innocent. Surely he had lived too short a time to be taught a horror of deformity? If I could take and educate him as my friend, I wouldn't be alone on earth!

And so, as the child passed, I drew him towards me. When he saw my face, he screamed and clapped his hands over his eyes.

I forced them away and said, "Child, I will not hurt you. Listen to me."

But he struggled. He called me monster. Ogre. He said I would tear him apart. Eat him. He said he would tell his papa.

"Boy, you will never see your papa again," I told him. "You must come with me."

"Let me go! My papa is M. Frankenstein. He is an important man, and he will punish you!"

"Frankenstein!" I exclaimed. "Then you belong to my enemy! I have sworn revenge on him. You shall be my first victim."

The child struggled and screamed and called me such vile names I grasped his throat to silence him. In a moment he lay dead at my feet.

As I gazed on him a hellish triumph swelled my heart. I too could create desolation and despair!

It was then I noticed something glitter on the child's breast. It was a painting of a most lovely woman, and I stared at it with delight. She had such kindness in her face! But then I realised that she too would only look at me with disgust and fright. I was once more overcome by rage and left my hiding place to find somewhere else to conceal myself.

I came to a barn which I thought empty. But no. A beautiful young woman was sleeping on some straw. Here, I thought, is another who would smile at everyone on earth but me. I bent over her and whispered, "There is someone here who would give his life for one kind look from you."

She stirred and terror ran through me. This young woman would wake and scream. She would do as everyone else did! I was driven to sudden madness. She shall suffer for the murder I have committed, I thought. I had learned from Felix how to work mischief. I placed the painting in her pocket and left.

And now, my creator, I face you. We will not part until you have promised to agree to my request. I am alone and miserable. Humankind will not associate with me. But a female as deformed and horrible as myself would not shrink away. I need a companion of the same species, with the same defects as myself. This being, you must create.

VICTOR FRANKENSTEIN

17.

I was bewildered by the monster's request, unable to understand him.

"You must create a female for me," the creature said again. "Someone with whom I can live in sympathy and understanding. This you alone can do. You cannot refuse me."

"I do refuse," I replied. "Create another like you? Together you would destroy the world! Be gone!"

He refused to leave. He wished to reason with me, he said.

"I am cruel because I am miserable," the monster explained. "If I had been accepted by mankind, I would have bestowed every kindness on him. But I am not. Even you, my creator, would happily tear me to pieces and not call it murder. If I cannot inspire love, I will inspire fear. You are my arch-enemy, and I will make you curse the hour of your birth!"

He burned with hellish rage but eventually calmed himself and continued.

"I intended to reason with you. This passion harms only me. You do not see or understand that you are the cause of it! Well then, I demand a creature as hideous as myself. We shall be monsters, cut off from the rest of the world. We will depend on one another. Our lives will not be happy, but they will be harmless. My creator, let me feel thankful to you for one thing. Do not deny me my request!"

I shuddered at the possible consequences, but there was some justice in his argument. He saw my change of feeling and said, "No human being would ever see us again. We will go to the vast wilds of South America. Acorns and berries will be our nourishment; dried leaves will be our bed. You have never pitied me, yet now I see compassion in your eyes. Will you not promise to do this thing I so desperately desire?"

I considered what he had said. "You propose to dwell in the wilds, but how can you? You long for the love and sympathy of man, so will never remain in exile. You will return and seek kindness. But wherever you go you will meet with the same revulsion. Your evil passions will be awoken, and you will then have a companion to assist you in destruction. You must not argue with me. I cannot agree to your request."

"How inconstant your feelings are!" the monster exclaimed. "A moment ago you were moved, and now you harden your heart against me. I swear to you that I will quit the world of men and dwell in the most isolated of places. My evil passions will vanish, for I will have the love and sympathy of my companion. My life will flow quietly away, and in my dying moments I shall not curse my maker."

His words had an effect on me. I wished to comfort him, but when I looked at the filthy mass of flesh that moved and talked, my heart sickened and I felt only horror. But could I really withhold from him a happiness that was in my power to give?

"You swear," I said, "to be harmless, but have you not already shown a hatred that should make me distrust you? Is this a trick to increase your triumph by gaining a greater opportunity for revenge?"

"What is this?" the monster asked. "I must not be toyed with. I demand an answer. If I am friendless and alone, hatred will indeed consume me. But there would be no cause for hatred or vice with a companion, an equal, a sensitive being at my side. I would have a purpose and a place in the world. A reason to exist."

I reflected on all he had said. I feared his power and his threat, and yet justice demanded that I should agree to his request. I turned to him and said, "I will do as you ask if you give me your solemn oath. You must leave Europe as soon as I have delivered a female to accompany you into exile."

"You will never see me again," the monster cried. "I swear by the sun and the blue sky of Heaven and by the fire of love that burns in my heart. Depart. Begin your labour. I will be watching. When your work is done, I will appear."

The monster left the hut, descending the mountain with the speed of an eagle, and was soon lost to my sight in the sea of ice.

His tale had taken most of the day, and the sun was already low on the horizon. I should have hurried, but my heart was heavy and my steps slow. Morning had dawned before I arrived back at the inn. Even then I took no rest but returned at once to Geneva where my worn and wild appearance alarmed my family. I hardly spoke to them. I had no right to their sympathy. To save those I adored I had to dedicate myself to a dreadful task. That task was now the only reality of my life; everything else was a dream.

18.

I could not find the courage to begin. I knew the monster watched me, and I knew he would be disappointed. I feared his anger but was unable to overcome my revulsion of the task that lay ahead.

I had studied anatomy for months before I had made my first monster, but only the male form. The construction of a female was complex and could not be done without me first undertaking further months of study. I had heard of new discoveries made by English scientists who possessed information that would be necessary for my success. I thought of asking my father if I might visit England, but I did not do it. I shrank from taking the first step, and as the days and weeks slipped by I began to wonder whether I should begin the task at all.

A change had taken place in me. My health was restored and I was in good spirits, as long as I could keep my unholy promise to the monster from my mind. When I could not, fits of sorrow seized me, turning sunshine to darkness. During these fits, I calmed myself with solitude, passing whole days on the lake, watching the clouds, listening to the rippling of the waves, letting fresh air and bright sun restore me.

One day my father called me to him. He had observed my changeable behaviour, wondered at its cause and come to his own conclusion.

"My son," he said, "I have always looked forward to your marriage with dear Elizabeth. From your earliest infancy you have always seemed entirely suited to one another. But you, perhaps, regard her as your sister and have no wish to have her as your wife. Indeed, you may have met another woman whom you love. I know you consider yourself honour bound to Elizabeth. Is this the cause of the unhappiness you struggle to overcome?"

I put my father's mind at rest, reassuring him that I loved Elizabeth and that I had every intention of marrying her. He then suggested that perhaps our wedding should be arranged without delay.

How was I to reply? It would be wise to finish the task I had promised before I considered my own happiness. I should waste no more time! I had to go to England, not only to meet its scientists but to find a place where I could begin my work. The female's creation could not be done in my father's house!

So I told my father I wished to take a pleasure trip to England. I would be absent for a few months or at most a year. When I returned, Elizabeth and I would be married. My father agreed to my plan; his only condition was that I should not go alone. I must be accompanied by Henry Clerval.

We left towards the end of August, travelling from Switzerland through Germany along the length of the Rhine. There was a great contrast between me and my companion. Henry was alive to every new scene. He enjoyed the setting sun and was even more happy when he saw it rise at the start of a new day. Clerval! Beloved friend! He had the heart and soul of a poet and a mind that was always bursting with fresh ideas and magnificent imaginings. He delighted in all the shifting colours of landscape and sky. While I, haunted by a curse, was a miserable wreck who could enjoy nothing.

We sailed from Rotterdam to England and on a clear morning towards the end of September, first saw the white cliffs of Dover.

Proceeding up the Thames we passed Gravesend, Woolwich, Greenwich. At last we saw in the distance the dome of St Paul's as our ship slid past the bloody Tower.

19.

In London, Clerval soon became friends with men of genius and talent. He was curious, sociable, keen to gain experience and learn from them.

I had once thirsted for knowledge for its own sake, but now I visited people only for the information they could give me.

Clerval was forever busy, and I encouraged him. In his absence I began to gather the materials necessary for my new creation.

We had arrived in London at the start of October. We left the city for a tour of the country at the end of the following March, travelling first to Windsor and from there to Oxford, where we stayed a considerable time. After that, to Matlock, Cumberland and Westmorland, where we remained two months before travelling on again.

All this time I neglected my promise to the monster. I feared his disappointment. I imagined him in Switzerland, revenging himself on my relatives, and waited for letters from home with feverish impatience. Each time the post was delayed I was overcome by a thousand terrors.

Sometimes I imagined that the monster followed me and would punish me by murdering my companion. When these thoughts came, I would not leave Henry's side, clinging to him like a shadow to protect him from his destroyer. I felt constantly guilty, as if I had committed some great crime.

We reached Scotland. I viewed Edinburgh with weary eyes and an exhausted mind. Clerval was full of cheerfulness and admiration, and enjoyed the beauty of the new city, the romantic castle, Arthur's Seat and the Pentland Hills.

After a week, we left Edinburgh for Perth, where an acquaintance had invited us to stay. But I was in no mood to talk or laugh or make plans for enjoyment. So I told Clerval that I wished to travel through the Highlands alone.

"I may be absent a month or two," I told him. "When I return, it will be with a lighter heart."

Henry was not happy, but I parted from my friend and set out determined to find some remote spot where I could finish my work in solitude.

The most distant of the Orkney Islands was the place I chose. It was hardly more than a rock, beaten by waves, with five residents whose senses were so numbed by poverty they paid me no heed. On the whole island there were only three miserable huts, and one was vacant. This I rented.

I devoted myself to my labours, which became ever more horrible as time passed. Sometimes I could not bear to enter my laboratory for days. At other times I worked through the night. It was a filthy process. An enthusiastic frenzy had blinded me to the horror of my task during my first creation. My mind had been fixed on achieving my goal. But now I was without that passion, and my heart sickened at the work of my hands. Once more I grew restless and nervous. I looked forward with eager hopes of freedom and happiness to the creature's completion. But those hopes were often overshadowed by dread of what evil might come.

20.

The sun had set. The moon was just rising from the sea. I sat in my laboratory, thoughts running through my head.

Three years ago I had created a devilish monster whose brutality destroyed my heart. I had given him a promise. I had done as he asked. And now my work was nearly complete.

I was about to give life to another being whose nature I knew nothing of.

It occurred to me suddenly that she might become more deadly than her mate. He was motivated by revenge. But she might enjoy murder for its own sake. He had promised to exile himself from mankind, but she had not. Would she consent to something that had been agreed before her creation?

They might hate each other! Suppose she turned away from him? What might he do if he was rejected by one of his own species?

Even if they went into exile together quietly and happily, what if they wished for children? They might spawn a race of devils who would threaten the very existence of mankind! In buying my own peace, did I have the right to inflict such a curse on the entire world?

I trembled.

Looking up, I saw the monster gazing in on me through the window, and my heart all but stopped beating. The light of the moon showed the savage cruelty in his face. It had been madness to create another being like him!

But I had not yet given the female the spark of life. And now I would not! With sudden passion I began to tear the thing apart. It took a matter of moments to destroy the creature. When the monster outside saw what I had done, he gave a howl of devilish despair and disappeared.

Hours passed. But at last I heard the paddling of oars and someone stepping from a boat. The door creaked. Footsteps came along the passage, and the monster appeared.

"How do you dare to break your promise?" he said. "I have suffered such toil and misery. I left Switzerland when you did. I crept along behind while you travelled in comfort. I have lived for months on the heaths of England and Scotland and suffered cold and hunger and fatigue. And now you destroy my hopes?"

"I do!" I said. "I will never create another like yourself."

"I have tried to reason with you. Remember I have the power to make you so miserable that even the light of day will be hateful to you. You are my creator, but I am your master now. Obey me!"

But I would not, and the monster saw my determination to refuse.

"Shall each man have a wife," he cried, "and each beast have a mate, yet I should be all alone? Are you to be happy while I live in misery? Only revenge remains to me now. I will die, but first you will curse the sun that shines on your sorrow. I will watch you with the cunning of a snake. You will regret what you have done tonight."

Once more I told the monster to be gone, and he departed, rowing across the sea with the swiftness of an arrow. But before he left he said, "I will be with you on your wedding night."

My wedding night? So that was the night my destiny would be fulfilled. I knew the monster would be satisfied only with my death, and the knowledge did not scare me. But when I thought of how bitterly Elizabeth would grieve for me, tears streamed from my eyes.

I walked around the island like a ghost as darkness turned to daylight. Violent rage gave way to despair and still I walked. The sun was low in the sky again when a fishing boat brought me a packet of letters. One was from Clerval, begging me to join him.

I decided to leave the island, but before I did so I needed to dispose of the female creature's remains. I could not leave them strewn about the floor for the islanders to discover! That evening I put the mangled flesh into a basket with a great quantity of stones. And at about three in the morning I put the basket into a little boat and sailed out from the shore. I cast it into the sea, listening to the gurgling sound as the basket sank.

A breeze then refreshed my spirits, and I decided to stay on the water awhile. I stretched myself at the bottom of the boat as I had so often done on Lake Geneva, and the waves soon lulled me into a sound sleep.

When I woke up, the sun was high, the wind was strong and there was no land in sight. I was lost upon the wide ocean.

Hours passed. I had no food. No water. No prospect of rescue. It was not until the sun was almost set that I saw a line of land and sailed south towards it. A little town came into view, and I steered the boat into the harbour.

A crowd had gathered, I thought to give me help. I was ready to sink from tiredness and hunger. But instead I got only hostile looks, and soon they were pushing me along the streets towards the magistrate. It seemed a man had been murdered the night before, and they thought I was to blame.

I remained perfectly calm, knowing myself to be innocent.

I did not expect the disaster that was about to overwhelm me.

21.

The magistrate was a kind man who listened calmly to the witnesses' evidence. The murdered man had been discovered on the beach by a fisherman who had thought at first that he must have drowned. But his clothes were dry and his body still warm. Black finger marks on his neck showed he had been strangled. A single man in a small boat was seen close by where the body was discovered.

When I heard of the finger marks, I trembled so much I had to lean on a chair for support.

The magistrate saw my reaction and assumed it betrayed my guilt. He took me to view the corpse so he could see the effect it had on me.

When I saw the lifeless body of Henry Clerval laid out in a coffin before me, I gasped for breath. Throwing myself on my friend, I exclaimed, "Have I taken your life too, dearest Henry?"

My body could not cope with the severe pain of mind and heart. I was seized by strong convulsions and carried out of the room unconscious. A fever came, and I lay for the next two months raving and on the point of death.

But I was doomed to live. After eight weeks, I woke as if from a dream to find myself in a prison cell. When I regained some sanity, the magistrate visited me.

"No doubt evidence of your innocence can be found," he said.

"That is the least of my concerns," I told him. "Death can be no evil to me."

"You have indeed been unfortunate," the magistrate said. "Thrown by accident onto this shore, charged at once with murder. Seeing the body of your friend, killed in so strange a manner and placed by some devil across your path."

We talked. I was surprised how much the magistrate knew of me. But it seemed that while I had been raving, the magistrate had examined my possessions and come across several letters, including one from my father. The magistrate had written to tell my family of my misfortune and of the charges that were laid against me. My dear father had travelled from Switzerland to be with me, as old and frail as he was. When he now entered the cell, I stretched out my hand to him and cried, "Are you safe? And Elizabeth? Ernest?"

My father calmed me and tried to raise my spirits, but a prison is no place to be cheerful. He looked at the barred window and sighed.

"You travelled in search of happiness, dear Victor, but death and disaster seem to pursue you. Poor Clerval!"

I began to weep. "Alas! I should have died on Henry's coffin, but I have a destiny that I must live to fulfil."

When the day of my trial came at last, it was proved that I had been in the Orkney Islands at the time Henry's body was found, and I was released from prison.

As we began our homeward journey to Switzerland the sun shone brightly and my father was in excellent spirits. But life was poison to me. I saw nothing but darkness.

22.

My father tried to rid me of my despair as we travelled, but there was nothing that could be said or done. I had killed Justine and William. And now Henry was dead, also by my hand. When I spoke my thoughts aloud, my father took them for the ravings of a madman and feared for my sanity.

We had reached Paris when I received a letter from Elizabeth. The darling girl expressed the same concern about our marriage as my father once had. She asked if she was the cause of all my unhappiness. Did I love another? Elizabeth assured me that she wished to be my wife, but if in marrying her I would make myself miserable, she would set me free.

Her letter reminded me of the monster's devilish threat.

I will be with you on your wedding night.

So be it, I thought. There would be a deadly struggle between us. If the monster won, I would be at peace. If I was the victor, I would be a free man.

Sweet, beloved Elizabeth! I read and re-read her letter and dared to dream of an earthly paradise with her. Yet it could not be. Like Adam, I had eaten an apple from the Tree of Knowledge and was now cast out of Eden. My death was certain. If I postponed our marriage, who knew what victims the monster might take before he came for me?

I wrote to Elizabeth, assuring her of my love. I told her also that I had a terrible secret that weighed heavily upon me and made me unhappy. I promised that I would reveal it to her the day after our wedding.

My father and I arrived home a week or so later. Ten days after that, Elizabeth and I were to be married.

Great God! If for one instant I had imagined the monster's hellish intention, I would have banished myself from home for ever.

I carried pistols and a dagger constantly, fearing he might attack me at any moment.

As the day of the wedding drew nearer, my heart sank within me. Cowardice? Terror? I don't know. I wore the appearance of cheerfulness, but Elizabeth saw beyond my smiles, and she too became downcast and sad.

The ceremony came and went. There was a party afterwards, but Elizabeth and I did not stay for it. Instead, we embarked at once on our honeymoon. We were to cross the lake that afternoon and continue on our journey the following day.

Our guests waved us off. Taking Elizabeth's hand in mine I said, "You are sorrowful, my love. But if you knew what I have suffered in the past and will endure in the future, you would try to make me happy on this one day."

"Dearest Victor," Elizabeth replied, "something tells me that I should not depend too much on the future that stretches before us. But I will not listen to a voice that is so sinister."

She smiled brightly. We sailed over the water, enjoying the beauty of the scene. They were the last moments of my life that I felt any kind of happiness.

The sun sank beneath the horizon as we landed, and all my fears returned – fears which would soon clasp me and cling to me for ever.

23.

It was eight o'clock when we landed. Elizabeth and I walked a short time on the shore in the twilight before retiring to the inn. That evening, the wind rose and a storm of rain came down.

I had been calm during the day, but night brought a thousand terrors. Elizabeth watched me in silence. I urged her to go to bed, thinking how terrible the coming struggle would be for her to witness.

She did as I asked, and I sat waiting, my hand on my pistol.

Waiting. Waiting. Waiting.

Hours passed. I was beginning to think that maybe some accident had befallen the monster and that he was not coming after all when I heard a shrill scream.

I froze. I could not move. But then the scream was repeated, and I rushed into the bedroom.

Why did I not die? Why does life cling closest where it is most hated?

Elizabeth lay across the bed lifeless, her head hanging down, her pale features half covered by her hair. The murderous mark of the monster's fingers was on her neck.

I bent over her in an agony of despair. And then, looking up, I saw the monster's grinning face at the window.

I fired my pistol, but he escaped, running with the swiftness of lightning and plunging into the lake.

The scream and the shot brought out a crowd of people who then went in pursuit of him with boats and nets. But they found nothing. No one.

A cloud of horror engulfed me. William, Justine, Clerval, and now my wife. And perhaps at this moment my father was writhing in the monster's grasp. Ernest might already be dead at his feet!

As soon as the storm passed I returned to Geneva to find my father and brother still lived. But when I told them what had occurred, my father was unable to cope with the grief of Elizabeth's loss. A few days later he died in my arms.

I went to the magistrate hoping that he might use his authority to pursue and capture the monster. I told him my whole story. He listened with kindness to begin with, but as it went on he began to doubt my tale. When I begged for his help, he tried to soothe me as a mother soothes a child when it wakes from a nightmare. Or a nurse soothes a raving lunatic.

I came away knowing that if the monster was to be punished, I would have to do it myself.

24.

I left Geneva intending to find the monster, but I didn't know which path to take. I wandered the streets, and as night fell I came to the cemetery where William, Elizabeth and my father were buried. Wind stirred the trees, but all else was silent. When I found their graves, my grief gave way to fury. They were dead, but I lived and so did their murderer. To destroy him I had to continue my weary existence. I knelt on the grass and kissed the earth.

I cried aloud to the heavens, swearing a solemn vow that I would live to take revenge. I called on the spirits of the dead to help me, almost choking with rage, and I roared, "Let the hellish monster drink deep of agony; let him feel the despair that now torments me."

I was answered by a fiendish laugh in the still night. It rang in my ears loud and long – the very mountains echoed with it. When it died away, the terrible voice whispered close to my ear, "I am satisfied, miserable wretch! You have determined to live, and I am satisfied."

I turned to see the rising moon shining full upon the monster's ghastly shape. He fled with more than mortal speed.

I chased him, and for many months this has been my only task. I followed the monster down the winding Rhône until he reached the Mediterranean, where by chance I saw him hide himself in a vessel bound for the Black Sea. I boarded the same ship, but he escaped from me. I followed in his tracks across the wilds of Russia. Peasants who had seen his awful form sometimes told me he had passed by. Sometimes he himself left some mark to guide me, no doubt believing I would despair and die if I lost all track of him.

When the snows descended, the monster would leave a single footprint on the vast white plain. Sometimes he marked the bark of trees. He even left me food so that I could eat and be refreshed. And once he left a message saying, "Follow me. I seek the everlasting ice of the north, where you will feel the misery of cold, but I will not. Come on, my enemy, we have yet to wrestle for our lives.

You must endure many hard and miserable hours before then."

Cold, hunger and tiredness were the least of the pains I suffered. Only in sleep could I taste joy, for then I saw and heard and spoke with my family and friends again. In sleep I saw all the beauties of my beloved country. The spirits that guarded me gave hours of happiness that helped me retain the strength to continue my pilgrimage. It was easy to persuade myself that my dreams were real and that my waking moments were but a nightmare.

I followed the monster ever northward, where rivers were turned to ice.

There I found another message from him: "Prepare! Wrap yourself in furs. Bring food. We shall soon embark on the journey that will satisfy my everlasting hatred."

Reading his words, I found courage. I called on Heaven to support me and continued to follow him across deserts of ice and snow. I bought a sled and dogs and travelled at speed. Little by little, I gained on him, and by the time I reached a tiny village on the ocean shore I was but a day behind.

There the inhabitants told me a gigantic monster had arrived in the night, stolen a sled and dogs and carried off their store of winter food. He had gone across the frozen sea in a direction where there was no land, and they thought he would soon be destroyed by the breaking of the ice.

I followed. And I cannot guess how many days have passed since then. Nothing but the burning desire for justice and revenge has carried me on. For many, many days there was not sight or sound or message from the monster.

And then one morning the dogs dragged me to the summit of an ice mountain. They struggled so hard that one of them collapsed and died. Despairing, I viewed the expanse before me and suddenly saw a dark speck upon the plain. A sled containing a figure of gigantic stature.

After two more days' pursuit, I came within a mile of him. I thought my journey was nearing its end. But then I heard thundering beneath the ice. The wind rose; the sea roared. With the force of an earthquake the ice split and cracked, and I was left drifting on a raft of ice.

Hours passed. One by one the dogs died. And then I saw your ship. Had you been going south I would have trusted myself to the seas rather than come aboard. But you, my friend, are northward bound.

If I die, Walton, swear to me that the monster shall not escape. I do not ask you to undertake my pilgrimage. Yet if he should appear when I am dead, swear he will not triumph. He is persuasive, and once his words had power even over my heart, but do not trust him. He is a liar with a soul as hellish as his form, full of spite and hatred. Call on the names of William, Justine, Clerval, Elizabeth, my father and the wretched Victor Frankenstein, and thrust your sword into his heart. I will hover nearby and direct the steel right.

CAPTAIN WALTON

It was the strangest tale. I had spent a week listening to Frankenstein, and when it was finished, we continued to talk. I found his company fascinating, for his mind was the match of mine. He would not reveal to me how he had given the spark of life to his creation in case I should be tempted along the same path towards self-destruction.

He spoke of his youth when he had thought himself destined for some great future, exactly as I did. Sometimes Frankenstein contradicted himself. He said he owed a duty to the monster he had created; that he should have tried to assure its happiness. Then he said he owed a stronger duty to his fellow men and had no choice but to refuse the monster's request for a companion.

He warned me of the dangers of over-ambition. Yet when the ship became trapped once more in mountains of ice and my men became mutinous and wished to turn for home, Frankenstein was furious and urged them to be heroes and not cowards.

His health declined day by day, although a feverish fire still burned in his eyes. He inched ever closer to death, and his shattered spirit found comfort only in his dreams, when he spoke with his friends. It was clear he believed them not to be the creations of his imagination but visitors from the spirit world.

It pained me bitterly to abandon my voyage of discovery. I would have rather died than return with my goal unfulfilled, but I could not proceed northward without the cooperation of my men. And so I gave them a solemn promise that if the vessel should ever be freed from the ice, we would return home.

When at last the sea began to move and a passage south was opened, the sailors gave a great cry of joy. And Frankenstein pressed my hand, a gentle smile upon his lips, and closed his eyes for ever. Death took him as he lay peacefully and quietly in bed.

At midnight I heard a voice coming from the cabin where Frankenstein's body lay. I entered and saw a gigantic creature looming over him.

A gigantic creature who appeared to be mourning his creator and begging his forgiveness.

I had promised to destroy the repulsive monster, but curiosity and compassion held me back.

"Why repent now?" I asked the monster. "If you had a conscience, Frankenstein would still live."

The monster turned on me. "You think I have no conscience? You think that I am a stranger to agony and remorse?" he said bitterly. "Do you think Clerval's groans were music to my ears? My heart was formed for love. You cannot imagine the pain I felt when misery pulled it towards vice and hatred. I was heartbroken by Clerval's murder. I pitied Frankenstein and loathed myself.

"But then I discovered that he dared to hope for happiness. He was to be married! Frankenstein wanted a comfort and companionship that he had kept from me for ever. Envy and rage overwhelmed me. All I wanted was revenge. The threat I had made about Frankenstein's wedding night became a promise. But I was a slave to the impulse, not a master of it, and I could not disobey. When Elizabeth died, I was not miserable. By then I had cast off all feeling. Evil became my good. Revenge was my unrelenting passion. But now it is ended. Frankenstein is my last victim."

For a moment I was touched with pity. Yet then I recalled what Frankenstein had said of the creature's powers of persuasion.

"Do you dare to complain about the sorrow you have caused?" I cried. "Hypocritical devil!"

"Your hatred of me cannot equal the hatred I direct against myself," he replied. "But my work is nearly complete. No one's death is needed now but my own. I shall leave your ship on the ice raft which carried me here and seek the northernmost point of the globe. I am polluted by crimes, torn by bitter regret. Where can I find rest but in death? Light, feeling, sense will pass away, and I will find happiness in oblivion.

"I shall make a fire that will devour this miserable body," the monster continued. "I will climb my funeral pyre in triumph and glory in the agony of the torturing flames. The light of that inferno will fade away; my ashes will be swept into the sea by the winds. My spirit will sleep in peace: or if it thinks, it will surely not think thus. Farewell."

The monster sprang from the cabin window onto the ice raft and was soon carried away by the waves and lost in distance and darkness.

Our books are tested
for children and young people by
children and young people.

Thanks to everyone who consulted on
a manuscript for their time and effort in
helping us to make our books better
for our readers.